THIS IS A HOSPITAL, NOT A ZOO!

by Roberta Karim
Illustrated by Sue Truesdell

Clarion Books / New York

Clarion Books
a Houghton Mifflin Company imprint
215 Park Avenue South, New York, NY 10003
Text copyright © 1998 by Roberta Karim
Illustrations copyright © 1998 by Sue Truesdell

The illustrations were executed in pen and ink with watercolor.
The text was set in 15-point Sabon.

www.houghtonmifflinbooks.com

Printed in Singapore

Library of Congress Cataloging-in-Publication Data

Karim, Roberta.
This is a hospital, not a zoo! / by Roberta Karim ;
illustrated by Sue Truesdell.
p.   cm.
Summary: Hospital patient Filbert MacFee transforms himself into a series
of animals to avoid some unpleasant medical procedures, making the nurses
so frustrated that he is finally allowed to go home.
ISBN 0-395-72099-0   PA ISBN 0-618-24622-3
[1. Hospitals—Fiction. 2. Animals—Fiction. 3. Nurses—Fiction.
4. Humorous stories.] I. Truesdell, Sue, ill. II. Title.
PZ7.K1384Wh   1997
[E]—dc20   94-43098
CIP
AC

TWP   10   9   8   7   6   5   4   3   2

For the nurses and doctors in our family, and Dr. J in Peds
R.K.

For Richard and Anna
S.T.

Six a.m.
All was still at Clovernook Hospital.

"One package for patient Filbert MacFee!"
The delivery man blasted his bugle.
The receptionist twanged to attention.
"Room 22," he said,
"and next time, use a flute."

Voices buzzed from Room 22.

"No more horseplay," said Head Nurse Beluga.
"Stop monkeying around," said Nurse Candy Z.
"But I feel much better,"
said Filbert MacFee.
"I'd like to go *home* now.
Please!"
Nurses Z. and Beluga shook their heads.
"More bed rest!" they said
as they zipped out the door.
"Bed.
        Rest."

FLUTE NOTES FLUTTERED IN FROM THE HALL.

"One package for Filbert MacFee!"
Filbert whispered,
"Finally!"
Quickly he popped an animal cracker
into his mouth and grinned.

get well
filbert

Nurse Skeeter darted in
to give Filbert a shot.
"Good morning, Patient Filbert MacFee!
Please roll over.
You'll feel a little pinch."
Patient Filbert replied,
"Oh no I *won't!*"
and turned into a . . .

RHINO.

"Hah *hah!*" he said.
"Try to put a needle through *that!*"

Nurse Skeeter rubbed his eyes.
"Nurse Beluga!" he called.
"Big problem in Room 22!"

Nurse Beluga marched into the room.

"A big problem, you say?
I'm bigger than problems.
I'm bigger than a hospital bed.
I'm bigger than 'most any patient around here!"
She frowned a big frown.
"What have you done with Filbert MacFee?"
"He's right here!" said Nurse Skeeter.
"Just a little . . . larger than life."
"I should say," said Nurse Beluga.
She took the rhino by the horn.
"Now listen here, you.
This is a hospital, not a zoo.
No
        rhinos
                allowed."

The rhino winced. "Ouch!" and

changed back to Filbert MacFee.
The shot rang true,
and the whole town knew.

NURSE CANDY Z. SAILED INTO ROOM 22.

"Nurse Skeeter is resting his eyes," she said.
"Now young man, time for your X-ray."
"Maybe later," Filbert said.
"It's warm and cozy under these blankets."

Nurse Candy said sweetly,
"Come sit in the wheelchair *this instant!*"
"But," said Filbert, "my gown is drafty."

Nurse Z. raised one eyebrow.
Nurse Z. raised both sleeves.
"Golly," said Filbert.
"I think she's been trained by Beluga."
Up in the air went Filbert.
Down to the wheelchair he flew.

"WHOO-HOO-HOO!" yelped Filbert.
"This chair is inhumanly cold!"

And he turned into a . . .

PENGUIN.

Nurse Z. raised two eyebrows.
"Penguin or not, you're still due in X-ray."
She flipped off the brake and wheeled him away.

"What have you done with Filbert MacFee?"
the X-ray technician asked.
"He's right here," said Nurse Z.
"His feathers are just a tad ruffled.
By the way, here's a note from Nurse Beluga."
The technician read the instructions.
He took the penguin firmly by the beak.
"Now listen here, you.
This is a hospital, not a zoo.
No
    penguins
        allowed!"

The penguin shivered. "Brrr!" and

changed back to Filbert MacFee.
Then they pressed him against
the ice-cold machine
and every ear heard
a full-bodied scream.

Nurse Wellington wheeled him back to Room 22.

"Nurse Z. is resting her ears," he said.
"Now young man, time for your medicine."
"No, thank you," said Filbert,
and sealed his lips tight.

Closer and closer came the shimmering spoon.
It could not be avoided.
He turned into a. . .

GIRAFFE.

"Tee hee HEE!" came the voice of Filbert MacFee.
"Just try to reach my mouth now!"

Nurse Wellington retreated.
"Nurse Beluga!" he called.
"Tall order for you
in Room 22!"

Nurse Beluga stomped down the hall.

"Tall order, you say?
I'm taller than orders.
I'm taller than elevators.
I'm taller than 'most any patient around here!"
She rounded the corner
and spotted the giraffe.
"I'm *not* taller than *that!*"

Filbert loomed near the ceiling.
Nurse Beluga shook her finger at Patient MacFee.
"Young man, this looming has got to stop.
I shall fetch a ladder."
A long neck followed her down the hall.

Nurse Beluga came back.
Filbert straightened up.
She parked the ladder at the bed
and climbed up, hand over hand.

JUST THEN, DR. KEBOB STOPPED BY ON HIS ROUNDS.

"What have you done with Filbert MacFee?"
Nurse Wellington handed him the chart.
"Well, well!" said Dr. Kebob.
"Not well at all!" said Nurse Beluga.
"This boy changes more than a hospital sheet."
She faced the giraffe.
"Now listen here, you.
This is a hospital, not a zoo.
No
        giraffes
                allowed!"

The giraffe kissed her nose
and changed into a. . .

GRIZZLY BEAR.

Nurse Beluga swayed in the air.
The bear snuggled under the covers.

Nurse Beluga climbed down and clenched her teeth.
"Bear or not, it's eight A.M.
Your pulse must be taken!"
She picked up a paw.
"Go away," growled the grizzly.
"I'm hibernating."

"Hibernating now, is it?" said Nurse Beluga.
She threw back the covers. "Winter is over!
And furthermore, Filbert,
this is a hospital, not a . . ."
"Oh bother," said the bear.
"I won't sleep a wink."
And he turned into an . . .

Dr. Kebob scribbled on the chart,
trying to keep up.

"Most interesting case," he muttered.
"Now Nurse Beluga,
can you change him back?"
"Now listen here, you,"
Nurse Beluga began.
"This is a hospital, not a zoo.
No
    orangutans
        allowed."

But the orangutan crouched low without a sound.
Nurse Beluga went nose to nose with the ape.
"Hallooooo in there!
What have you done with Filbert MacFee?"
The orangutan blinked one giant tear.

"Oh dear," said Nurse Beluga.
"What have I done to Filbert MacFee?"
She patted dry his tear.

Dr. Kebob crouched to examine the patient.
"Ouch!" he grunted. "My knees!"
The orangutan grunted back, happily.

His furry arm slid under the pillow
and brought out a cracker for Dr. Kebob.

"For me?" said the doctor.
"Don't mind if I do."
And he changed into . . .

an orangutan too.

They went eye to eye.

"Ooh-ooh-OOH," said the first.

"Ahh-hah-HAH!" said the second.

41

Together they leapfrogged Nurse Beluga
and swung above the bed.

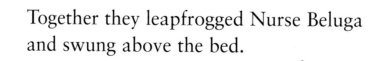

She straightened the hair on her head
and said,
"Now see here, you two!
This is a hospital, not a zoo."
The apes rolled their eyes, and
changed back.

patient: MacFee, F.

"Your diagnosis, Doctor?" asked Nurse Beluga.
"*What* do we do with Filbert MacFee?"
Dr. Kebob listened hard with his stethoscope
and gave the thumbs-up sign.
"Filbert's all better,
except for *one thing*."
"What now?" asked Nurse Beluga.
"Homesickness!" said Dr. Kebob.
"That's a *big* problem," said Nurse Beluga.
"Bigger even than me."
"Filbert MacFee?" said Dr. Kebob.
"Yes, sir?"
"*You* may go *home*!"

Filbert bounded down from the bed.
He handed out hugs
and crackers
all around.

Then Filbert MacFee
changed out of his pajamas,
and rode straight home on a . . .

LLAMA.